Shadows and Ghosts

GOTHIC POEMS FROM THE MIDNIGHT GUNN REALM

THE MIDNIGHT GUNN SAGA

C. L. MONAGHAN

To the loyal souls who journeyed far and wide,
Through Midnight's realm, where shadows abide.
In pages dark and tales untold,
Your presence shines like gleaming gold.
With hearts of courage and minds of grace,
You ventured forth, to find your place.
In Midnight's world, where mysteries unfurl,
You've left your mark, a precious pearl.
So to you, dear readers, with love profound,
This dedication, in echoes resound.
For without your light, our tales would dim,
To Midnight's realm, forever we'll hymn.

Introduction

In the realm of shadows, where ghosts doth tread,
A collection of verse, where darkness is fed.
"Shadows and Ghosts" unveils secrets untold,
In the Midnight Gunn realm, where mysteries
    unfold.
Within these pages, Gothic poems arise,
In the depths of night, where darkness lies.
Midnight Gunn's world, both haunting and vast,
Is captured in verse, from present to past.
From Draugr's revenge to the Peckham Vampire's
    jest,
Each poem reveals a tale, put to the test.
With Gredge by his side, and Polly in tow,
Midnight Gunn navigates a world in shadow.
So journey with us, through London's despair,
In "Shadows and Ghosts," where Midnight does
    dare,
To explore the darkness, the secrets, the fright,
In the realm of Midnight Gunn, where day turns
    to night.

Josephine

In realms unseen, where fae and mortals dwell,
Lies a tale of love, of heaven and of hell.
Josephine, born of Oberon and Mab's embrace,
A child of light and darkness, a queen's grace.
From the Otherworld she fled, her heart aflame,
Seeking solace in lowly mortal's name.
Josiah Gunn, a man of flesh and bone,
Captured her heart, her spirit to atone.
In mortal guise, she walked the earth,
A love forbidden, a bond of worth.
With Josiah by her side, she found her place,
In the mortal world's fleeting embrace.
But fate is cruel, its hand unkind,
And on the day a solar eclipse, intertwined.
As Haley's comet streaked across the sky,
Josephine breathed her final sigh.
In childbirth's agony, she passed from life,
Leaving Josiah to bear the strife.
With Midnight in his arms, a legacy of love,
He mourned his lost Josephine, his soul's dove.
From that day forth, he wandered alone,

Haunted by memories, by love overthrown.
A man consumed by grief's relentless tide,
For his beloved Josephine, his heart's guide.
So let us raise a toast to love's embrace,
To Josephine and Josiah, in time and space.
Though death may part them, their love remains,
Entwined forever, in eternal chains.

Death's Dark Shroud

Hush says the cold of death's dark shroud,
Wherein, Josephine lies, her spirit unbowed.
With Midnight cradled in her arms so tight,
She whispers farewells into the night.

Her breath grows shallow, her heartbeat fades,
As darkness descends, in eerie cascades.
She holds him close, with a mother's love,
Praying he'll find solace, in the heavens above.

But as her strength wanes, her grip grows weak,
And tears stain her cheeks, so pale and meek.
For she knows she must leave him, alone in this
    world,
Her heart heavy with sorrow, her fate now
    unfurled.

Through the veil of tears, she gazes into his eyes,
A silent goodbye, as she softly sighs.
She watches him sleep, so innocent and pure,
Her love for him, eternal, forever to endure.

And as her life ebbs away, into the night,
She holds onto him, with all her might.
For in his tiny hands, she finds her peace,
Her love for him, a bond that will never cease.

So as the shadows claim her, and the night grows
*   cold,*
Josephine's spirit, will forever enfold.
In Midnight's grace, her legacy lives on,
A mother's love, in the darkness, eternally drawn.

Josiah Broken

The stillness of the night entombed, Josiah weeps,
His heart heavy with sorrow, his grief runs deep.
For Josephine, his love, his light, now gone,
Leaving him adrift, in a world so wrong.
Through empty halls and echoing rooms,
He wanders aimlessly, consumed by gloom.
Her laughter, her smile, now but a memory,
As he grapples with the pain of her loss, so dreary.
The world around him carries on, unchanged,
But Josiah's world is forever rearranged.
For in his heart, there's an empty space,
Where Josephine's love once found its place.
He longs to hear her voice, to feel her touch,
But she's gone now, beyond his clutch.
And so he mourns, in the silence of the night,
Lost in a sea of darkness, longing for light.
For Josiah's grief knows no bounds,
As he searches for solace, in the depths of his sounds.
But even as the world moves on, he remains,
Haunted by memories, trapped in his pain.

Shadows Kiss

In the sigh of an evening's tender embrace,
A child of glow and of gloom finds his place.
Midnight Gunn, with eyes ablaze and soul afire,
Torn between light's promise and shadows' desire.
Tempestuous childhood, a tumultuous ride,
As powers of light and darkness collide.
A thousand needles pierce his tender young flesh,
As blackness beckons with silent, haunting mesh.
Tempted by the pulsating call of the night,
He walks the path of darkness, devoid of light.
Yet with each step, the pain becomes a balm,
A blissful agony, a whispered psalm.
The shadows' caress, so intoxicating,
A seductive dance, ever captivating.
But in the depths of darkness, he finds no release,
Only the promise of pain, without surcease.
And so he turns to the blessed light,
A healing fix, in the depths of night.
With each ray, he feels his spirit soar,
As shadow recedes, to haunt him no more.

For in the tempest of his soul's dark plight,
He finds solace in the blessed light.
A beacon of hope, amidst the gloom,
Midnight Gunn, in the healing light, finds room.

Victoria's London

Victoria's London, where fog shrouds the day,
Lies a world of mystique, where ruffians play.
Through dimly lit streets and alleys decrepit,
Whispers of vice and corruption are cryptic.
In rookeries hidden, where poverty thrives,
Desperation breeds, where hope barely survives.
Opium dens beckon with their siren call,
Where souls are lost in a haze, doomed to fall.
Petty crimes abound in the dark of the night,
Thieves and cutpurses, seeking fortunes slight.
Beneath gaslit lampposts, they ply their trade,
In the underbelly of a city decayed.

But high above, in mansions grand and fair,
The aristocracy breathe a different air.
They see London as a jewel, gleaming bright,
A beacon of progress, in their lofty sight.
To them, the rookeries are but distant tales,
A world apart, where society pales.
Their balls and galas, a glittering facade,
Masking the truth of a city remarkably flawed.

Yet even in their opulent halls of power,
Darkness lurks, in every hidden hour.
For London's secrets, both low and high,
Bind the city together, under the sky.
So let us peer through the veil of time,
To Victoria's London, in its prime.
A city of contrasts, both dark and fair,
Where darkness dances with secrets to share.

Twilight's Realm

Twilight's realm of softly spreading shadows
    prance,
Prowls a lord with powers most unconfined.
Midnight Gunn, his presence a mystical trance,
With secrets veiled, his destiny now defined.

He wields the night, its darkness his domain,
A master of shadows, bending to his will.
With whispered words, he weaves a web arcane,
His every move with potent magic fill.

Yet burdened by the gift of sight unseen,
He feels the weight of every whispered lie.
The hearts of men, their sorrows, joys, and spleen,
Revealed to him beneath the moonlit sky.

Despising peers who revel in the night,
Alone he stands, a solitary king.
In solitude, he finds his truest light,
A silent guardian with clipped, blackened wing.

So let him roam in solitude's embrace,
Lord Midnight Gunn, in shadows find his grace.

Scotland Yard

In the heart of the city, amidst the clamour and
    chaos,
Stands a bastion of order, a sentinel of justice:
Scotland Yard, its stone façade weathered by time,
Its corridors echoing with the whispers of history.
Within its hallowed halls, men of purpose and
    determination,
Navigate the labyrinth of crime and deceit,
Their minds sharp as the blades they wield,
Their resolve unyielding against the tide of villainy.
Behind closed doors, strategists pore over maps and
    documents,
Piecing together the puzzle of nefarious deeds,
Their pens scratching out the names of the guilty,
Eyes ever watchful for the faintest glimmer of truth.
In the dimly lit interrogation rooms,
Suspects sweat under the scrutinising gaze of
    detectives,
Their alibis unraveling like threads in a tapestry,
As the weight of justice bears down upon them.
Outside, the streets of London pulse with life,

But within the walls of Scotland Yard,
A different rhythm prevails,
The rhythm of duty, of honour, of justice.
For in this citadel of law and order,
No crime goes unpunished, no villain escapes,
And as the sun sets over the city,
Scotland Yard stands as a beacon of hope,
A testament to the resilience of the human spirit,
And the triumph of righteousness over darkness.

Limehouse Lament

In the flood of Victorian London gloom,
Lies Limehouse, a district cloaked in doom.
Where gaslit streets weave a tangled maze,
And secrets linger in the fog's murky haze.
Theatres echo with tales of woe and despair,
As actors tread boards, their souls laid bare.
Their words a lament, their faces a mask,
As they dance with demons in the shadows they
    bask.
Taverns teem with the desperate and forlorn,
Seeking solace in spirits, their souls ever torn.
Ale flows freely, a balm for the weary,
But beneath the laughter, the mood is eerie.
Opium dens beckon with their siren song,
Promising oblivion, a place to belong.
In smoky rooms, the lost souls reside,
Dreams consumed by the opium tide.
And in the alleys, beneath the gaslight's gleam,
Lurk the fallen angels, with faces unseen.
Prostitutes ply their trade, their bodies for sale,

In a world where love is but a fairytale.
In Limehouse, darkness reigns supreme,
A realm of vice, a twisted dream.
Where sinners and saints walk hand in hand,
Bound by the shadows of this cursed land.

Green Fairy

A magical moment of emerald hue,
Absinthe whispers secrets, old and new.
Its scent, aniseed's sweet symphony,
Unveils the world in vibrant tapestry.
A muse for poets, artists' delight,
Absinthe's elixir ignites the night.
With every sip, reality bends,
In verdant swirls, imagination sends.
Opal visions, minds ascend,
Through veils of green, they comprehend.
The worries of the world, they dissolve,
In absinthe's embrace, problems resolve.
Within its depths, illusions play,
Where truth may bloom in subtle array.
Oh, sweet elixir, guide our flight,
To realms where dreams and truths unite.

In the mystic realm where dreams take flight,
The absinthe fairy twinkles in the night.
With wings of jade and mischief in her eyes,
She leads the way to where imagination lies.

Beneath her gaze, reality bends and sways,
In her laughter, secrets find their ways.
But heed her charm, for she's a fickle sprite,
In her whims, crosses the line twixt dark and light.
Yet in her dance, there's a truth untold,
In the absinthe's embrace, mysteries unfold.
So let us follow where the fairy leads,
To where the emerald elixir feeds.

One Fateful Night in Peckham

In the murky depths of a city night,
Where sinners lurk in glowing moonlight,
Gredge and Midnight, a duo bold,
Hunt for a vampire, fierce and cold.
With stakes in hand and hearts afire,
They track the fiend, never to tire.
Through winding alleys and streets unknown,
They chase the creature to its evil throne.
But lo and behold, what do they find?
A man of means, with a twisted mind.
An aristocrat, with a penchant for blood,
His Transylvanian accent, a theatrical flood.
He welcomes them with a sinister grin,
As they stand in shock, unable to begin.
For here stands the vampire they sought,
But not the creature of legend they thought.
With a laugh that echoes through the night,
The aristocrat reveals his plight.
A lover of drama, with a flair for the stage,
He's simply a man, trapped in his own cage.
So Gredge and Midnight, in disbelief,

Realise their hunt has come to a cease.
For the Peckham Vampire, feared by all,
Is nothing more than a gentleman's drawl.
They bid him adieu with a shake of the head,
As they turn to leave, the vampire's dread.
For in this tale of darkness and humour,
Even the hunters can become the rumoured.
But alas, the man's antics didn't end there,
For he found himself in the asylum's care.
His Transylvanian dreams, now locked away,
In the confines of madness, he'll forever stay.

Ode to a Nightingale

In shadows deep, where dark deeds are spun,
Lurks a villain, a fiend rivaled by none.
Hemlock Nightingale, with eyes aglow,
A soul as black as the night's shadowy flow.
With cunning wit and a devil's grace,
He sought the key to an eternal place.
Harnessing the essence of a demon's might,
He plotted to conquer eternal night.
Through mechanical wonders of his own design,
He forged his tools, a sinister sign.
Goggles of glass, imbued with demon's breath,
To seize souls of the innocent, their impending
    death.
His silver claws, he wore, his talons of might,
To reap the souls, and thieve their light.
From the living he stole, leaving shells behind,
Empty vessels, devoid of heart and mind.
With each soul claimed, his power grew,
A tyrant of darkness, his will anew.
For in the depths of his villainous soul,

Lies the desire for eternal control.
But beware, oh mortals, of Hemlock's grasp,
For his thirst for power knows no gasp.
In the realm of shadows, where evil's gleam,
Hemlock Nightingale reigns, a darkling dream.

The Little Match Girl

Huddled, cold on a dreary street,
Here wanders Polly, with silent, weary feet.
A match girl orphan, with naught but her dreams,
Amidst the shadows, where hope gleams.
Her hair a cascade of curls, dark and wild,
A contrast to the sorrow that's left her beguiled.
With a cheeky grin, she faces the night,
A flicker of defiance, a spark of light.
But tragedy has marked her tender years,
A hand lost to sulphur's bitter tears.
Yet still she perseveres, with courage untold,
In a world where kindness is rare as gold.
With muck-spout mouth, she'll spin her tales,
Of princes and castles, of ships and gales.
For in her imagination, she finds her escape,
From the hardships of life, the sorrow, the ache.
Though the streets may be cruel, and the nights may
*   be long,*
Polly's spirit remains steadfast and strong.
With a matchstick in hand, she'll light up the dark,
A beacon of hope, a tiny spark.

So let us remember this orphaned maid,
Whose resilience and spirit will never fade.
For in the heart of a child, amidst pain and strife,
Lies the power to kindle the flame of life.
Alone she sits by the old dockyard,
Little Polly, in the winter's hard.
Half frozen, with matches unsold,
In the bitter cold, her fate foretold.
Her small hands tremble, her breath a mist,
As she clings to hope, in the frosty midst.
With nowhere to turn, no shelter in sight,
She shivers in the darkness, longing for light.
Her tiny frame, so frail and weak,
In the snow she lies, unable to speak.
With each passing moment, her spirit fades,
As the winter's chill envelops her in shades.
But in her eyes, a flicker of light,
A spark of hope, in the darkest night.
For even in despair, she holds onto dreams,
Of warmth and love, amidst the icy streams.
So let us not forget, in the winter's snow,
The little match girl, with nowhere to go.
For in her plight, we see our own,
A reminder of the kindness we've shown.
And as she fades into the winter's embrace,
Let us remember her, in a moment's grace.
For in her innocence, lies a lesson learned,
Of compassion and love, forever earned.

Widdershins

In the heart of the forest, where shadows reign,
Widdershins prowls, a creature of disdain.
With eyes that gleam in the moon's pale light,
He hunts in the darkness, in the dead of night.
Through tangled trees and whispering leaves,
He moves with a silence that deceives.
His fur, a cloak of midnight hue,
Conceals the horrors that he'll pursue.
With each step taken, the forest groans,
As Widdershins claims it as his own.
Beneath the moon's watchful eye,
He seeks his prey, with a wicked cry.
But beware, for those who cross his path,
Widdershins brings terror and wrath.
In the depths of the forest, where daylight quells,
He reigns supreme, a creature from hell.

The Barghest's Redemption

In whispering woods where moonlight wanes,
Roams a mythical beast with tortured chains.
Widdershins, once Rowland, by fate undone,
Cursed by the hand of Mab, the Unseelie one.

A Barghest grim, with fur of night,
His howls pierce through the shroud of fright.
Through tangled brambles, he prowls unseen,
A spectre of dread, in realms between.

In ancient lore, his name was sung,
A harbinger of death, from whence he sprung.
But in his soul, a flicker remains,
A glimmer of hope, amid despair's domains.

For in his heart nestled 'neath the boughs,
A child named Polly, his guardianship allows.
To her, he's sworn, by oath and by vow,
To protect her innocence, from darkness now.

In her laughter, he finds a fleeting light,

A beacon in the depths of endless night.
With every step, he guards her close,
Defying the shadows, where fear enclose.

Yet, echoes of his past still haunt his soul,
The blood he's spilled, the toll he stole.
Can redemption be found in this forsaken plight,
Or is he doomed to roam, eternal night?

Through mist and mire, he'll tread the path,
Beside young Polly, shielding her from wrath.
For in her innocence, he sees a chance,
To redeem his sins, through valour's dance.

But as the stars fade in the dawn's grace,
Widdershins knows, he's bound by fate's chase.
A creature of darkness, with a heart entwined,
In the tale of Polly, his redemption he'll find.

Laura's Plight

In a mansion veiled by mysteries deep,
Where secrets lie and spectres creep,
There dwells a maiden, fair and meek,
Whose heart is bound, yet doomed to seek.

Laura, the housemaid, her spirit confined,
By chains of duty, her love enshrined.
Her Master, Midnight Gunn, with eyes of coal,
Rescued her soul from infernal toll.

In the depths of despair, her life did wane,
Till Midnight's hand snatched her from pain.
Saved from the grip of demonic consumption,
She owes her existence to his redemption.

But alas, in the gloom of the grand estate,
Their love blooms forbidden, sealed by fate.
For she is but a servant, lowly and plain,
While he, a master, in societal reign.

Her heart aches in silence, a torment untold,

For love's embrace, be it forever cold.
Though passion's flame ignites her soul's flight,
Society's chains bind her love from sight.

Oh, how she longs for his tender caress,
To share a love forbidden, yet no less.
But reality's sting cuts deep and true,
Their romance condemned, before it could brew.

With heavy heart and tear-stained eyes,
Laura knows the truth, amidst love's lies.
To stay would mean perpetual sorrow,
In the shadows of their love, with no tomorrow.

So, with trembling hands and aching sighs,
She bids farewell, beneath moonlit skies.
Leaving behind the man she adores,
To seek solace in far away distant shores.

In the depths of night, she wanders alone,
A love forsaken, a heart turned to stone.
For Laura, the housemaid, her fate is sealed,
In the annals of love, her story revealed.

Beware the Pooka

In the gardens of St. Francis, where roses bloom,
Lies a realm of secrets, a mystics boon.
Here the Pooka roam, in the moon's low light,
Their forms shifting, a haunting sight.

With eyes aglow and hooves that gleam,
They beckon to mortals, with a whispered scheme.
In voices of rhyme, they weave their spell,
Promising riches, but beware the toll.

For the Pooka's bargain is a dangerous game,
With consequences dire, and souls to claim.
They lure you with promises, sweet and fair,
But beneath lies darkness, a trap laid bare.

In the dead of night, they gallop and prance,
Through the corridors of dreams, in a wild dance.
Their laughter echoes, a chilling sound,
As they tempt you to tread on unhallowed ground.

But heed this warning, oh mortal soul,

Beware the Pooka's treacherous goal.
For though their words may tempt and beguile,
Their price is steep, their motives vile.

So if you encounter these creatures of dread,
Flee from their grasp, or you'll end up dead.
For in the gardens of St. Francis, they reign,
And to cross their path is to invite pain.

Dark Duo

In the still of the night, secrets are kept,
For Gunn and for Gredge, their vigil adept.
Whispers of crimes, both unearthly and dark,
Echo through London, leaving a mark.
With Midnight's sight, beyond mortal ken,
They hunt the fiends that dwell within.
Gredge's grit, matched by Midnight's might,
Their resolve unyielding, in the grip of fright.
Through winding streets and shadowed lanes,
They chase the phantoms, where darkness plays.
For where others falter, they stand tall,
In the face of evil, they'll heed the call.
In the silence of London, where mysteries lie,
Gredge and Midnight, beneath the sky,
They'll unravel the enigma, piece by piece,
Their bond unbroken, their quest won't cease.
In the heart of the city, where temptations dance,
Gredge and Midnight, in a delicate trance.
A detective of logic, a mystic of lore,
Bound by fate, forevermore.
Together they walk, through the streets they roam,

In pursuit of justice, they make their home.
Gredge with his logic, Midnight with his sight,
Their partnership forged in the depths of night.
For where Gredge sees clues, Midnight sees signs,
In the whispers of shadows, in the arc of designs.
Their methods may differ, but their goal remains
    clear,
To vanquish the darkness, to quell the fear.
In the alleys of London, where secrets abide,
Gredge and Midnight, side by side.
A testament to friendship, forged in strife,
In the tapestry of darkness, they are life.
In the labyrinthine alleys of the mind,
Gredge and Midnight, their destinies entwined.
Amidst the echoes of the unknown,
They navigate the shadows, together grown.
With Gredge's logic and Midnight's sight,
They pierce the veil of the endless night.
In the depths of London's darkest hour,
They wield their power, with ardent fervour.
For where Gredge sees facts, Midnight sees fate,
In the tapestry of time, they collaborate.
With every step, they unravel the past,
In the pursuit of justice, they'll stand steadfast.
In the whispers of the wind and the shadows'
    embrace,
Gredge and Midnight, the formidable chase.
For in the heart of darkness, they'll shine the light,
Guiding London through the endless night.
In the heart of London, where darkness reigns,
Midnight Gunn, a figure draped in veils,
His eyes ablaze with an unearthly glow,
Guided by whispers from long ago.
Beside him stands Detective Gredge, austere,
In Midnight's realm, a steadfast pioneer.

Together they tread through the city's decay,
Unveiling secrets hidden away.
In alleys dim and cobblestone streets,
They chase the spectres where evil meets.
Midnight's powers, a force to be reckoned,
Unraveling mysteries, divine and beckoned.
As shadows deepen and mysteries unfold,
Gredge and Midnight, a bond untold,
For in the depths of London's darkest night,
They are the guardians of justice's light.
In the depths of London's labyrinthine sprawl,
Gredge and Midnight heed the city's call.
With Gredge's logic and Midnight's sight,
They navigate the darkness, banishing the blight.
Through alleys dim and forgotten lanes,
They chase the spectres, where evil reigns.
For where Gredge sees evidence, Midnight sees
    more,
In the shadows of the city, their bond they explore.
With every crime, they unravel the tale,
In the heart of the darkness, they'll prevail.
For Gredge and Midnight, a partnership divine,
In the annals of justice, they'll eternally shine.

Ghostly Guardian

Deep in the country, where mortals ne'er creep,
Lies a burial mound, where the Draugr sleeps.
Guardian of treasure, keeper of the past,
He awakens to revenge, when thieves trespass.

With eyes ablaze and a heart of stone,
The Draugr rises from his ancient throne.
His bones encased in armour of old,
A ghost of vengeance, fierce and bold.

For in the depths of his slumber deep,
He hears the whispers, the secrets they keep.
The thieves who dared to steal his kin's gold,
Their fate sealed by the Draugr's hold.

Through mist and fog, he hunts them down,
In the darkness of night, they'll surely drown.
No mercy for those who disturb his rest,
For the Draugr's wrath is fierce, his revenge the test.

With each step, he closes the gap,

His presence a curse, a shadowy trap.
No mortal hand can halt his stride,
For the Draugr's fury knows no guide.

And so, beware the burial mound's keep,
Where Draugr lie in eternal sleep.
For those who seek to steal their gold,
Shall face the wrath of vengeance untold.

The Saga Unfolds

Deep in the depths of fog-laden streets,
Where blackguards and villains constantly meet,
There lies a tapestry woven with care,
Of characters bold, in a world so rare.
First, there's Midnight Gunn, with eyes aglow,
A mysterious soul in the city's shadow.
Born of Josephine and Josiah's embrace,
He walks the line between two worlds' grace.
Beside him strides Detective Gredge, austere,
A man of logic, in Midnight's small sphere.
Together they roam through the city's gloom,
In pursuit of justice, dispelling doom.
Amidst the alleys and cobblestone lanes,
They encounter a tale of ancient remains.
The Draugr, a guardian of the past's might,
Rises from slumber to reclaim the light.
In the burial mound's darkened embrace,
He seeks revenge, with a ghostly face.
Against thieves who dare to disturb the peace,
He brings justice to the realm's unease.
Then there's Polly, an orphaned match girl,

In Midnight's world, a glistening pearl.
With curls dark as night and a spirit bright,
She adds a touch of innocence to the fight.
And in the shadows, where secrets abide,
Widdershins prowls, his presence implied.
A Barghest grim with fur of night's hue,
He guards Midnight's path, loyal and true.
Amidst these characters, a story unfolds,
Of darkness and light, of secrets not told.
In the heart of London, where mysteries hide,
Their epic saga stretches far and wide.

A Tale of Meriton

In Meriton House, on Berkeley Square,
Midnight's mansion, beyond compare.
Giles Morgan, the butler true,
Serves with loyalty, through and through.

Clementine Phillips, with scones divine,
Her cooking skills, a cherished sign.
In the heart of the home, where warmth abounds,
Midnight's household, where love resounds.

Oh, Meriton House, where secrets hide,
In the depths of darkness, and shadows bide.
But in the parlour, by the fire's glow,
Midnight finds solace, in the brandy's flow.

In the library, with tomes arcane,
Midnight delves, his knowledge to gain.
The occult sciences, his passion's flame,
In ancient texts, he seeks his name.

Giles, his confidant, by his side,

In Midnight's lair, where magic resides.
In the basement's depths, where memories creep,
Midnight ponders, in silence deep.

Oh, Meriton House, where mysteries lie,
In the whispered tales, where spirits sigh.
But in the parlour, where embers dance,
Midnight finds comfort, in his trance.

Through the halls of Meriton House, they roam,
In the heart of London, their true home.
Together they stand, through thick and thin,
In Midnight's mansion, where stories begin.

Oh, Meriton House, where legends grow,
In the chambers dark, where dreams bestow.
But in the parlour, where flames inspire,
Midnight finds peace, in the brandy's fire.

Wee Bonnie Castle

In Scotland's wilds, where winds doth wail,
Stands a castle old, a haunting tale.
Its walls, like sentinels, whisper tales of old,
Of knights and ladies, brave and bold.

Creaking oak doors, with hinges worn,
Guard secrets of the past, where spirits mourn.
And creeping vines, with tendrils bold,
Take hold of the castle, its heart to mould.

Midnight's purchase, an ambitious endeavour,
To breathe new life, and to make it clever.
For in its halls, where echoes ring,
Lies ancient magic, fit for a king.

Amidst the ruins, a stone circle stands,
A portal to the Otherworld's lands.
Where fae do dance and spirits roam,
In the castle's air, old magic's home.

With each step taken, Midnight feels,

The ancient power, the castle's reels.
For in its heart, where shadows play,
Lies the promise of a brighter day.

With hammer and chisel, he'll restore its grace,
Bring back the glory, to its rightful place.
For in this castle, amidst the wilds,
Lies the magic of Midnight's wiles.

Halfblood in Hiding

The halls of the British Museum, bright and
    grand,
Within strides Miss Elldy Bird, with knowledge in
    hand.
With her hair tinged purple, a curious sight,
A blend of fae and human, her heritage alight.
Her face, kindly, her grace no-nonsense indeed,
As she tends to the artefacts, with scholarly heed.
In pantaloons she roams, on a bicycle swift,
To her, the archives are a precious gift.
The archives are her haven, her sanctuary of old,
Where ancient artefacts their stories unfold.
With fae blood coursing through her veins,
She guards their secrets, amidst history's chains.
With every artefact she handles with care,
She feels the magic, lingering there.
For Miss Elldy Bird, with her keen eye and wit,
Knows that history's tales are not quite writ.
For in the halls of the British Museum, grand and
    tall,

Strides Miss Elldy Bird, with knowledge enthral.
With her unique lineage blend, a story to unfold,
In the museum's hallowed halls, her tale is told.

43

Strides Miss Elldy Bird, with knowledge enthral.
With her unique lineage blend, a story to unfold,
In the museum's hallowed halls, her tale is told.

A Glimpse of Romance

In the depths of the museum's ancient halls,
Where artefacts whisper and history calls,
Detective Gredge and Miss Elldy Bird,
Find their hearts entwined, their feelings stirred.
Through corridors of knowledge, side by side,
They share moments fleeting, in quiet stride.
With each artefact they explore and trace,
Their growing affection finds its place.
In the mysteries they unravel, hand in hand,
They discover a bond, both strong and grand.
For in the shadows of the museum's embrace,
Love blossoms, in this sacred space.

The O.U.I.

Released from the dim-lit chambers of Scotland
 Yard,
Gredge stood free, his resolve iron-hard.
Years of service behind him, a detective renowned,
But a yearning for change, in his heart, profound.

With a nod and a farewell, he left behind,
The familiar walls, the memories enshrined.
To open his office, a venture anew,
The Office for Unusual Investigations, true.

By his side, Miss Elldy Bird, with knowledge vast,
Together they delved, into the mysteries amassed.
In the depths of the archives, they sought to uncover,
The secrets that lay hidden, waiting to be
 discovered.

Their first case, a tale of a cursed necklace's blight,
Whispers of tragedy, in the dead of night.
With determination in their hearts, they pursued
 the trail,

Piecing together clues, without fail.

Through dusty tomes and ancient lore,
They followed the threads, seeking more.
In the heart of the city, where shadows fall,
They unravelled the mystery, standing tall.

For in the Office for Unusual Investigations'
    domain,
Arthur Gredge and Elldy Bird, together they reign.
With each case they solve, their bond grows strong,
In the world of the unusual, now where they belong.

Down in the Vaults

The museum's vaults, where dark things dwell,
Lies a treasure trove of secrets, with stories to tell.
Ancient artefacts, shrouded in mystery's cloak,
Whispers of the past, from days of yore they evoke.
Each object holds a tale, a fragment of time,
A glimpse into a world, lost in the sublime.
From crumbling scrolls to sacred relics old,
The archives hold secrets, waiting to be told.
In the darkness of the basement, they lie,
Guardians of secrets, beneath the watchful sky.
Their magic lingers, in the dust-filled air,
Enchanting all who dare to venture there.
The echoes of the past, reverberate still,
As the artefacts whisper, their tales to instil.
Of lost civilisations, and forgotten lore,
Of heroes and villains, and so much more.
So if you dare to wander, into the museum's depths,
Beware the artefacts, for they hold secrets kept.
For in their silent vigil, they guard the ancient way,
In the museum archives, where legends may stay.

Ode to Charlie

In the stables where a young soul dwells,
There lies a tale that no one tells.
Of young Charlie Fenwick, a soul once lost,
But now found, at Midnight's cost.
Saved from the clutches of Hemlock's grasp,
By Midnight's courage, in darkness vast.
Now he serves with pride, in livery bright,
A groom and driver, in the fading light.
With a smile on his lips and laughter in his eyes,
He brings joy to Polly, under moonlit skies.
In the carriage he drives, with steady hand,
Through the streets of London, a noble stand.
But beneath his cheer, a shadow lingers,
Nightmares of Hemlock, with icy fingers.
For the memories haunt him, in the dead of night,
A constant reminder of darkness's might.
Yet still he stands, with courage true,
In service to Midnight, through and through.
For in the face of fear, he finds his strength,
A testament to resilience, in life's great length.

So here's to Charlie Fenwick, with livery bright,
A beacon of hope, in the darkest night.
In Midnight's service, he finds his place,
A soul redeemed, in the light's fair grace.

49

A Song for Agnes

(Verse 1)

In the mansion's halls, where nightmares dance,
Stands Miss Agnes, with a haunted glance.
Her family lost to the Boo Hag's wrath,
She carries their memory, along her path.
Blonde and beautiful, with eyes of blue,
Yet haunted by fears, in the night's dark hue.
A governess to Polly, her charge so dear,
She shields her from troubles, with love sincere.

(Chorus)

Oh, Miss Agnes, with your heart so brave,
In the face of fear, you stand unfazed.
Through the gloom and the long night's unrest,
You protect Polly, with love, the best.

(Verse 2)

From the land across the sea, she came,
To London's streets, where she laid claim.
But in her heart, a secret fear,
That the Boo Hag's grasp, draws ever near.
With each passing night, she watches and waits,
For the whisper of danger, at the mansion's gates.
Yet she stands strong, against the night's dread,
Protecting Polly, with words unsaid.

(Chorus)

Oh, Miss Agnes, with your courage true,
In the face of danger, you see it through.
Through the darkness and the night's unrest,
You guard Polly, with love, the best.

(Bridge)

Though the Boo Hag's shadow looms overhead,
Miss Agnes holds firm, with strength she's bred.
For in her heart, she knows the truth,
Love's light shines brightest, in the dark's uncouth.

(Chorus)

Oh, Miss Agnes, with your spirit bright,
In the face of danger, you shine a light.
Through the shadows and the night's unrest,
You guide Polly, with love, the best.

Escape

Through the forests and islands of the deep South,
Midnight and Widdershins, pursued by a mouth
That thirsted for blood, a relentless Boo Hag,
Her fury unyielding, her presence a drag.

Through swamps and bayous, they fled her wrath,
But the Boo Hag's pursuit left them in her path.
With each step they took, she drew ever near,
Her hunger for their souls, a terror to fear.

In the dark of the night, they sought to escape,
But the Boo Hag's power, they could not break.
Her claws like daggers, her eyes ablaze,
They were trapped in her grip, in a desperate daze.

With nowhere to run, they faced their demise,
But Widdershins, so cunning, saw through the lies.
He opened a portal, to the Otherworld's gate,
And through it they fled, before it was too late.

But little did they know, what fate had in store,

For Midnight was captured, his freedom no more.
In the realm of Queen Mab, he now resides,
A prisoner of darkness, where shadows abide.

Through forests and islands, their journey's tale,
A harrowing escape, where courage prevailed.
But in the clutches of darkness, Midnight now lies,
A captive of fate, beneath starlit skies.

A Plot of Vengeance

Heed the deep depths, where malice reigns,
Midnight languishes, in Queen Mab's domain.
Her dungeon cold, a prison grim,
Where Midnight's spirit, grows ever dim.
For Mab, with cunning, holds him tight,
Blackmailing him with threats of blight.
His beloved Polly, her pawn in the game,
His heartache deepens, his soul aflame.
Yet in the darkness, Midnight finds,
His powers growing, his spirit entwined.
With every passing day, he schemes and plots,
For vengeance burns, in his deepest thoughts.
For Queen Mab's hold, though strong it seems,
Cannot quench the fire, of Midnight's dreams.
With each flicker of his darkening power,
He plans his escape, his finest hour.
Through shadows deep and darkness vast,
Midnight plots, his freedom at last.
For though Mab's grip may hold him tight,
His spirit soars, in the depths of night.

So let Queen Mab beware, and mark my words,
For Midnight's revenge, shall fly like birds.
In the realm of shadows, where he bides his time,
His escape draws near, his vengeance prime.

55

Midnight Acrostic

Mysterious whispers in the night, a cloak of darkness worn,
In shadows deep, where secrets keep, Midnight Gunn is born.
Darkness and light, entwined in his soul's embrace,
Night's silent guardian, in the depths of time and space.
In the heart of London's streets, where shadows loom and play,
Gazing upon the world with eyes that see both night and day.
Hidden depths, a realm unknown, where magic's power lies,
Underneath the moon's pale glow, Midnight Gunn defies.
Gathering secrets, weaving tales, in the midnight's hush,
Unraveling mysteries, in the silence's gentle brush.
Navigating through the darkness, with courage in his heart,
Noble and true, with each step, playing his part.

Polly's Villanelle

In Polly's eyes, a gift unseen, she sees,
Auras swirling, colours bright and bold,
A window to the soul, where truth's keys tease.

With every glance, she feels the gentle breeze,
Of energies that shimmer, uncontrolled,
In Polly's eyes, a gift unseen, she sees.

In hues of blue and gold, her mind agrees,
To read the secrets that the aura holds,
A window to the soul, where truth's keys tease.

Through joy and pain, her vision freely flees,
Revealing hearts, their stories yet untold,
In Polly's eyes, a gift unseen, she sees.

Yet burdened by the weight of mysteries,
She walks the path where shadows darkly fold,
A window to the soul, where truth's keys tease.

Though oftentimes her soul feels ill at ease,
She knows her gift is precious, to behold,
In Polly's eyes, a gift unseen, she sees,
A window to the soul, where truth's keys tease.

58

One Lonely Yule

Meriton House, in mourning deep,
A somber hush, where silence seeps.
Polly sits alone, on Christmas Eve,
In the empty halls, where memories grieve.
The fireplace stands, with ashes cold,
No warmth to chase away the bitter bold.
Beside it hangs his empty stocking,
A reminder of the loss, her heart still locking.
The armchair sits, in the dim firelight,
Where he once sat, in the dead of night.
His absence echoes, in the empty space,
A void that time cannot erase.
And at the dinner table, a chair left bare,
Where he should sit, with a knowing stare.
But he's gone now, lost to the night,
Leaving Polly alone, in the fading light.
In Meriton House, where grief doth dwell,
Polly's heart aches, in a lonely spell.
For Christmas without him, feels so bleak,
In the darkness of loss, she's afraid to speak.

Night Stalker

Widdershins, a creature of the night,
With eyes that gleam in the moon's soft light.
In shadows black, he pads with grace,
A silent guardian of a hidden place.
His fur, a cloak of midnight hue,
Conceals the secrets he holds true.
In the forest's depths, alone roams he,
A mystical being, wild and free.
But beware, for his loyalty is strong,
To those who've earned his trust, he'll belong.
With every step, he guards the night,
Widdershins, a creature of dark delight.

The Wolf

Widdershins,

Shadow's faithful,

Guardian of the night's secrets,

Mystical protector roaming,

Ever.

Laura's Dream

The tortured chambers of her heart, Laura finds
    solace,
Amidst the shadows that linger,
In the presence of Midnight, her sanctuary.
His gaze, a beacon in the darkness,
Guiding her through the tumult of emotions,
Drawing her closer, like a moth to flame.
In his arms, she finds refuge,
A haven from the storm raging within,
His touch, a balm to her wounded soul.
With every whispered word, every tender caress,
Laura's love for Midnight blooms,
A delicate flower, fragile yet resilient.
For in the depths of her heart,
Midnight's love is a flame that burns bright,
Illuminating the darkness that once consumed her.

Midnight's Elegy

The realm of Midnight Gunn, where shadows
  prance,
A tapestry of tales, a world of chance.
Through haunted halls and forest's deep,
The echoes of sorrow and secrets we keep.
In Meriton House, where mysteries reside,
Midnight stands, with instinct as his guide.
With Widdershins by his side, a loyal friend,
Their bond unbroken, until the very end.
From Laura's love, a flame that burned,
To Gredge's courage, forever earned.
Miss Elldy Bird, with fae blood intertwined,
In the darkness of London, her light shined.
Through trials and tribulations, they endured,
In the face of darkness, their spirits assured.
But in the end, as shadows fall,
Their memories linger, within us all.
For in the realm of Midnight Gunn's world,
Their stories told, their banners unfurled.
A legacy of courage, love, and strife,

Forever remembered, in the tapestry of life.
In the heart of the Gunn Household's walls,
Miss Agnes Carmichael, her voice calls.
Haunted by ghosts, her courage held true,
Protecting Polly, in the darkness, they grew.
And Charlie Fenwick, with livery bright,
In Midnight's service, he found his light.
Though haunted by nightmares, of Hemlock's
*   reign,*
His loyalty unwavering, through joy and pain.
And, Midnight himself, in his dungeon cold,
Where threats linger, and stories untold.
His spirit unbroken, his will strong and true,
Plotting his escape, vengeance in view.
In the realm of Midnight Gunn, their stories
*   entwine,*
A pillar of courage, in darkness they shine.
Though shadows may fall, and darkness may loom,
Their legacy lives on, in the evening's gloom.
But whispers echo in the darkness, foreboding and
*   grim,*
A sense of impending doom, a future dim.
For Midnight's escape, though plotted with care,
May lead to consequences, beyond compare.
In the Otherworld's depths, where shadows wane,
A reckoning awaits, where powers reign.
For Queen Mab's hold, though weakened it seems,
May unleash a fury, beyond Midnight's dreams.
And as the shadows deepen, and the night grows
*   long,*
The fate of Midnight Gunn, hangs in the throng.
But amidst the darkness, a glimmer of hope,
A flicker of light, a way to cope.
For in the hearts of those who dare to fight,

A spark ignites, against the darkest night.
And though the future may be shrouded in mist,
Their courage and strength, cannot be dismissed.

Farewell

As shadows fade and twilight ages,
Our journey ends, within these pages.
But in the echoes of the night,
Our tales live on, in soft moonlight.
To all who've journeyed with us here,
Through joys and sorrows, laughter, and fear,
We bid farewell, but not goodbye,
For in these pages, our spirits lie.
Thank you for the moments shared,
For the dreams we dared, for the burdens bared.
May the echoes of our stories linger on,
In your hearts, long after we are gone.
So as the stars begin to fade,
And dawn breaks through the night's cascade,
Remember us, in shadows deep,
For in your dreams, our souls will sleep.
Farewell for now, dear readers all,

Until we meet again, at Midnight's call.

Also by C. L. Monaghan

Visit My website

The Midnight Gunn Saga

The Hollows: A Midnight Gunn Novel- 1

The Barghest: A Midnight Gunn Novel- 2

The Draugr: A Midnight Gunn Novel- 3

The Boo Hag: A Midnight Gunn Novel- 4

The Immaginario Duet

Immaginario- 1

Andato- 2

Cancer Charity Poetry Book

Steel Petals 'Voices'

Future Releases

The Half Bloods: A Midnight Gunn Novel- 5

The Midnight Gunn Victorian Grimoire & Bestiary

Shadows of Midnight Torn

Lailoken: First Mage

The Heather Bleeds

The Wyfe and The Warding

Solomon's Seal"

Born and raised in the industrial landscapes of Lincolnshire, UK, Monaghan's literary journey has traversed continents, from the adventurous terrains of South Africa, where she experienced the thrill of cheetah kisses, to the vibrant book events across the pond in the United States.

Monaghan's academic prowess is reflected in her B.A. honours degree in History and English literature, a rich tapestry that feeds her creative spirit. Her novels, characterised by paranormal romance and Gothic mystery, have garnered critical acclaim and numerous accolades. Notably, her works achieved finalist positions in their genres at the IAN Book of the Year Awards in 2017 and the Readers' Favourite Awards in 2018, marking her excellence in the craft of writing.

As an avid reader, Monaghan draws inspiration from literary giants such as J.R.R. Tolkien, Enid Blyton, Stephen King, Terry Pratchett, and her friend and mentor, the late indie author Ednah Walters. It was Walters who encouraged Monaghan to write the stories she wanted to read. Thus, the debut novel "Immaginario" was born, bringing to life Monaghan's own book boyfriend.

A self-proclaimed Scotophile, Monaghan now resides in the enchanting landscapes of Scotland with her husband and home-schooled children. True to the writer's stereotype, her household includes a cat named Slinky and, Casper and Loki, the miniature schnauzers. Monaghan's passion lies in crafting dark, dastardly historical and gothic tales that not only capture the imagination but also enthral the soul.

In an exciting venture, Monaghan has become part of the BooksOffice book-to-screen TV project, a testament to her literary prowess. With dreams as expansive as her storytelling, she aspires to elevate her novels, especially those featuring the mysterious wealthy anthropologist Lord Midnight Gunn, into a household name and a popular TV series, enchanting audiences with the enigmatic allure of her narratives. As the pages of C.L. Monaghan's novels turn, a world of mystery and Gothic wonder unfolds, inviting readers to embark on a journey where darkness and romance dance in perfect harmony.

In her recently launched podcast, "The Writer's Lathe," C.L. Monaghan warmly invites listeners to embark on a captivating journey into the depths of her creative realm. Explore the intricate tapestry of influences that shape her craft, as Monaghan skilfully unravels the threads of writing, history, mythology, and the supernatural. With profound insights, she reveals the alchemy that occurs in her creative process, where these diverse elements converge to lay the foundation for crafting exhilarating and best-selling Gothic mystery novels.

Visit My Website